A Home for Molly

A Home for Molly

Holly Webb
Illustrated by Sophy Williams

SCHOLASTIC INC.

For Mia

Text copyright © 2015 by Holly Webb
Illustrations copyright © 2015 by Sophy Williams

All rights reserved. Published by Scholastic Inc., *Publishers since 1920*.
SCHOLASTIC and associated logos are trademarks and/or registered
trademarks of Scholastic Inc. Published by Scholastic Inc., 557
Broadway, New York, NY 10012.

This book is a work of fiction. Names, characters, places, and
incidents are either the product of the author's imagination or are
used fictitiously, and any resemblance to actual persons, living or dead,
business establishments, events, or locales is entirely coincidental.

ISBN 978-1-338-13967-9

10 9 8 7 6 5 4 3 2 1   17 18 19 20 21

Printed in the U.S.A.   40
This edition first printing 2017

Chapter One

Anya lay on her front in the sand, trying to build a tower of pebbles. It was quite tricky because she was holding a turkey sandwich, so she only had one hand free for building. She was a bit full for another sandwich, really, but because they were on vacation, her mom had let her have potato chips with them so she didn't want to waste it.

"Anya, do you want a drink?" Mom called over from the picnic blanket. "And some cake?"

"In a minute," Anya murmured. She balanced a large black stone on top of her tower and looked at it hopefully. It wobbled for a second or two—and then the whole thing collapsed. Anya sighed, but she didn't mind that much. It was the fifth time she'd built it and it always fell down in the end. This tower had been higher than any of the others. She got up and wandered back over to the picnic blanket, where her mom and dad were trying to persuade her little sister, Jessie, that she was too small for cake. Jessie was only nine months old, but she was convinced that everybody else's food was nicer than hers. Anya thought she was probably right—some of the meals in the baby recipe book sounded very odd. Who would want to eat Tasty Lentil Surprise?

Anya took her drink and a slice of cake and moved over to the edge of the blanket so that Jessie couldn't see her. Otherwise it would just be mean.

The beach was really busy today. Anya looked around at all the other families, who were mostly eating their lunches, too. Anya's family had only come to the beach for a quick visit the day before, when they'd first arrived in Saltmere. There had been unpacking to do and Jessie had been a bit tired after the long car journey. This was their first proper beach day. Anya hadn't felt lonely yesterday—it hadn't been the real start of their vacation. But today... She couldn't help wishing that she had someone else to build sand castles with—or make mermaid statues with, like those three girls over by the steps up to the promenade. Or even swim with—there was a whole big family group standing by the edge of the water now, the children squeaking at the coldness of the waves washing over their toes.

"Oh, *look*..." Anya whispered as the family's dog splashed through the water, too. She darted into the waves and then shook herself all over the children, making them squeal.

"They're so lucky," Anya murmured to herself. The dog was gorgeous, even when she was wet. Anya wasn't really sure it was a girl dog, of course, but the dog was so pretty—golden brown and curly all over, with great fluffy ears and a sort of topknot of blond fur. The seawater had turned her curly fur into coiling tendrils all over. She wasn't very big, and Anya wondered if she was still a puppy.

She watched the family splashing with one another and playing with the dog while she tried to build her tower of stones again. She couldn't help feeling a bit jealous. There was an older boy, a girl about her age, and a littler girl as well. They were all laughing and flicking water at one another.

Anya sighed and looked around at Mom and Dad and Jessie. Her little sister was cute and Anya adored her—most of the time. But it was going to be quite a while before Jessie would be big enough to play in the sea with her.

And the other family had a gorgeous fluffy puppy, too! Anya loved dogs and she really wished they could have one of their own. Dad had said maybe—when Jessie was bigger. He'd had a dog when he was Anya's age and he loved them, too. But he said he didn't think a dog was a great idea with Jessie being so tiny—and grabby. Even the nicest dog would get grumpy if Jessie pulled at its ears, he pointed out, and Anya had to admit that he was right. Jessie was always pulling her hair and it hurt, even though Jessie didn't mean it to.

The children were coming out of the sea now, heading back to their spot farther along the beach by the steps. Anya could see their mom and dad waving. The fluffy little golden dog was racing along the beach after them, stopping to sniff here and there. Anya giggled as she saw the puppy gobble down a bit of sandwich that someone had dropped and then sniff at a pile of seaweed. She looked like she might be about to eat that, too, and Anya wondered if she ought to tell the children. Seaweed wasn't the sort of thing that would be good for a dog to eat. Anya frowned disapprovingly as they hurried back to their parents along the beach. How could they not notice that their dog had been about to eat something disgusting? She couldn't help thinking that if *she* had such a lovely dog, she would take better care of it than that.

But then the golden puppy stopped nibbling at the seaweed and raced after the children, flinging herself at their legs and yapping. The older girl was just walking past Anya and her tower of stones, and the little dog was so excited that she knocked it over with her wagging tail.

"Oh! I'm really sorry!" the girl said, looking down in horror at the pile. "I didn't mean to knock it over."

"It's OK! It was an accident. The dog knocked it with her tail," Anya said a little shyly. "She's beautiful."

"She is, isn't she?" the other girl agreed, watching as the puppy chased off after her little sister. "She's called Molly. Do you want me to help you build your tower again? I was looking at it as we came past—it was really tall! I bet I couldn't do that, but I could pass you the stones or something?"

Anya smiled at her. "Don't worry. I was only building it because I was a bit bored. It falls down every time. I must have built about seventeen towers by now."

"You're bored?" The girl looked very surprised. She glanced around the beach, as though she couldn't see how anyone could be bored in such a nice place.

"My dad says he'll come in the sea with me later," Anya explained. "But right now he's looking after my baby sister and giving my mom a break. And he says it's not a great idea to go in the sea on my own. I suppose I could paddle, but ..." She shrugged. "You're so lucky having your brother and sister to play with."

The other girl sat down next to Anya and let out a huffy sigh. "You think? Didn't you see Zach tip me up into that wave? Having a big brother is *awful.*" She sniffed. "Little sisters are a bit better, but Lily always wants to do everything I'm doing, which is a real pain sometimes." She grinned at Anya and nodded over at Jessie. "You'll find out! But I suppose I am quite lucky, really. It wouldn't be as much fun here without them to do things with." She glanced back at Anya. "You could come and build sand castles with us, if you like. My mom says the tide's going to be high in an hour, so if we want to get the water to go around the castle, now's the time to build it. Would your mom and dad let you?"

Anya nodded. "I'm sure they would. I'll ask. Um, thanks," she added, turning red. "That's really nice of you."

"I'm Rachel," the girl said, jumping up. "I'll come with you. Then I can show your mom and dad where all our stuff is. We were going to build our castle just over there."

Anya's mom was delighted that she'd found someone to play with.

"Of course you can," she said, smiling at Rachel. "It's very kind of you to let Anya join in. Are you the same age as Anya? Nine?"

"I'm almost ten," Rachel said. "And my brother, Zach, is twelve and Lily's seven. They're both over there." She pointed across the beach. "Oh, they've started. We'd better go, or Zach will build it all wrong."

Anya picked up her spade and followed Rachel over to her brother and sister. Zach was already digging enthusiastically, making a channel for the sea to flow into the moat, and Lily was collecting stones and seashells to decorate the castle. Molly was helping her, sniffing at the piles of seaweed again and rooting shells out for her to pick up.

Anya and Rachel started to build the main part of the castle, digging out a deep moat and piling the sand into the middle to make the fort. Every so often, they had to stop and shoo away Lily, who kept trying to stand on the mound of sand.

"I'm bigger than you!" she sang to Rachel.

Rachel rolled her eyes. "Yes, Lily, *because you're standing on a big pile of sand*!"

Anya giggled, and Rachel shrugged at her. "Just you wait," she muttered, elbowing Anya in a friendly sort of way. "Oh, look, look! The water's starting to come in!"

A creamy yellow foam was creeping slowly down Zach's channel, and the girls danced up and down excitedly, waiting for it to get right into the moat.

"This wave! It's going to be this one!" Anya yelped. "Look! There it is! Oh, no ..."

Molly had been watching the water most suspiciously, glaring at it as it inched along. Now she leaped into the moat and stood there barking at it, sand showering down from the castle all over her golden coat.

"You're going to need a bath tonight," Anya giggled. "Come on! Come on!" She coaxed the little dog out and sat down next to her, patting her gently as they watched the water spread all around the moat. Rachel crouched next to them and stroked Molly's ears.

"Yay, look, it's meeting in the middle!"

Rachel squealed, jumping up and nearly falling in the moat herself, before sitting back down again.

Anya gave the surprised puppy a hug and then laughed as Molly licked her chin. "I'm so glad you knocked down my tower," she whispered in Molly's curly ear.

Chapter Two

Molly lay on the sand between Anya and Rachel, her eyes half-closed. One of the girls was scratching her behind the ears, just where she was itchy, and the sun was warm on her back. She could feel that she needed brushing to get the sand and salt out of her coat, but she was warm and comfortable, so she didn't mind.

"Want to play cricket?"

Molly twitched her ears and looked up as the girls began to talk over her head. The boy was standing there with a ball, so she jumped up with an excited little woof.

"Oh, she wants to play!" said Anya. "Do you like chasing balls, Molly?"

"As long as she doesn't eat my tennis ball," Zach said doubtfully. "Still, I suppose she can fetch it if Lily hits it into the sea!"

"I won't!" Lily yelled, stamping her foot, and Molly edged back, looking worried.

"Oh, she's scared. Careful, Lily, you frightened her, shouting like that. Good dog, Molly." Rachel crouched down and fussed over her, and Molly licked her hand gratefully. She didn't like it when people were loud. But she soon forgot that she'd been scared as she raced around for the ball, barking excitedly as the children laughed and chased after her.

"She's the best fielder I've ever seen," Zach said, grinning. "Come on, Molly. Give me the ball! Come on—oh, no, Molly! I could have gotten Rachel out if you hadn't held on to it."

"She's on our side," Rachel said smugly. "Good dog, Moll. Oh, look, Mom's got biscuits. I'll give you one when she's not looking."

Molly wagged her tail blissfully and wolfed down the sweet biscuit, looking hopefully over to the girls for more.

Anya giggled. "Oh, go on, then. You can have half of mine—I'm not that hungry. I suppose you're growing—you need the energy!"

Molly gobbled the biscuit and flopped down on Anya's feet, sleepy after all the racing around that she'd done. She was still hungry, of course, but the biscuits had been very, very good.

It was one of the best afternoons that Anya had had in ages. But all too soon, Rachel's mom and dad were rolling up their blankets and sending everyone to find the spades and bodyboards and balls that they'd left scattered over the sand.

"Will you be back on the beach tomorrow?" Rachel asked hopefully, and Anya nodded. She'd wanted to ask the same thing, but what if Rachel didn't want her hanging around with them again?

"Oh, Rachel, I think we might

be going to that adventure park tomorrow," Rachel's mom said, looking up from packing away all the damp swimming things. "We're not quite sure. But maybe we'll see you the day after, Anya?"

Anya nodded and smiled, then wandered back to Mom, Dad, and Jessie.

"Weren't they friendly?" her mom said, smiling. She'd chatted with Rachel's mom and dad for a bit when she'd come over to check on Anya.

"They probably aren't coming to the beach tomorrow, though." Anya sighed, flumping down onto the sand next to Mom.

"Well, I owe you a swim. We'll definitely do that tomorrow," Dad pointed out. "It's getting a bit chilly now that the wind's picking up. Might be time to think about going back to the cottage. Don't worry, Anya. I promise you'll have fun tomorrow. I'll take you in the sea, and we could bring the kite down, too."

Anya smiled at him. Dad was right—she would love going in the sea for a proper swim. It was just that everything seemed a bit quiet and flat now without Rachel and the others.

"I've just thought of something," Dad said, looking worried.

"What?" Anya asked anxiously—Dad was really frowning.

"We've been on the beach for a whole day and none of us have had ice cream!"

"Oh, Dad! I thought something terrible had happened!" Anya grinned.

"That *is* terrible! Come on. Help me fold up the picnic blanket and we'll go to the ice-cream shop on the way back."

Molly watched as the children trailed away along the path up to the top of the cliff, laden down with bags and buckets and sandy shoes. They had fussed over her and petted her all afternoon, and for the first time in ages she had felt as though she had really belonged to someone. But now they were going and she was left behind again.

She had tried to follow them, but the older girl had shooed her back. "Go on,

Molly! Go home! Go and find your owners—that's them over there, isn't it? Those boys?"

Molly gave a hopeful whimper and tried again, trotting along behind them, but the man had pushed her gently back toward the beach and told her no. She knew they wouldn't let her stay, even if she did sneak after them again.

So she went back to the beach and sat by the little kiosk that sold the ice cream and beach toys. They had a bowl of water outside for dogs, and she was thirsty after running around in the sun all afternoon. The kiosk sold bacon rolls and sandwiches as well, and she'd found leftovers in their trash cans before. But she couldn't go scuffling through them until later on, or the owner would shout at her and chase her away.

"That's such a cute little dog," a girl said as she came away from the kiosk, with an ice cream cone. "I wonder who she belongs to."

The girl's mother looked over at Molly and smiled. "Oh, she's with that family sitting down by the steps. I saw

31

them playing with her. She is sweet, isn't she?"

The beach was emptying out now, just a few people left and all of them were slowly packing up their things. The families with beach huts began to put away their chairs and tables, and Molly watched them hopefully, wondering if there would be any scraps left when they'd gone.

The lady who ran the ice-cream kiosk came out to fold up her shutters, and Molly skittered away behind one of the beach huts before the lady could shout at her. She scurried along behind the line of huts and came out by the steps. She would go and sniff along the line of broken shells and seaweed down by the sea. She'd found things to eat mixed up in there before.

Molly dragged her paws over the deep sand, feeling weary. She had loved playing with the children that afternoon, but now she was worn out and so hungry. The seaweed smelled strong and salty and there was another smell—a hopeful sort of smell. A fish! She scrabbled at it excitedly with her paw and it broke up into bits.

Molly sneezed at the smell—it had been dead for a while and didn't smell very nice. It was dry and leathery from lying there all afternoon in the hot sun. She could just about remember the delicious bits of fish she used to get as a treat when she'd lived with her owners, before she was a stray—this fish smelled quite different. But Molly was too hungry to be fussy. She wolfed it down, even the bones and the dried-up skin.

After the fish, Molly padded along the sand to the little hollow under the patch of grass. This was the wilder end of the beach, past the concrete promenade, where the road led down to the harbor. It was never as busy, so there wasn't as much chance of scraps from a picnic. But the dunes were a quiet place to sleep. Molly had found a sandy hole under a big clump of grass a few weeks before. She'd then dug it out a little more, so that it made a nest just large enough for a small dog to sleep under cover. She snuggled into it and curled up. Her stomach was hurting— the fish probably hadn't been a good thing to eat. But it had been all there was.

Chapter Three

The next day, Anya and her parents packed the picnic things under Jessie's stroller again and got ready to set off for the beach. Anya had been hopping about by the front door for what seemed like ages. When they'd stopped at the ice-cream shop the day before, she had spotted a bodyboard with dolphins on it, and she'd been admiring it while the lady behind the counter scooped out their ice cream. The dolphins were very gorgeous—they looked as though they were smiling, and Anya couldn't help smiling back at them. Then she'd heard Dad saying, "And we'll take that bodyboard as well, please."

Anya had wheeled around, staring at him in surprise. She hadn't even asked, just thought how much fun it would be to have one. Lots of the people on the beach that day had been splashing around on them.

Now she was desperate to get down there and try it out. It just seemed to be taking forever for Mom and Dad to finish sorting out the picnic and Jessie's things. Anya had run around finding all of her sister's toys, but now Jessie needed her diaper changed.

Eventually, Dad lifted the stroller over the front step, and they set off along the clifftop path to the beach.

"Looking forward to trying out your bodyboard?" he asked, watching Anya admire the dolphins again as she carried it along.

"It's going to be awesome," Anya told him as she tried to squash down the thought that it would be even more fun with a friend. Still, she had Dad to swim with, which was going to be fun, too. He often worked really late, so Anya didn't see him that much except on weekends and during vacations.

As soon as Dad had helped spread

out the picnic blanket and unload all their picnic stuff, he and Anya picked their way over the pebbles and sand down to the sea. It was a beautiful hot day and the water was calm.

"The sea is really blue today," Anya said, sounding surprised. "Yesterday it was sort of browny-green."

"Maybe it's reflecting the sky," Dad suggested. "Are you ready for this, Anya?" He grinned at her. "You don't want to back out?"

"No!" Anya glared at him. "Although it does look cold," she admitted.

Dad tested the water with one foot. "Ugh. Make that very cold."

"Go on!" Mom called. She was standing farther up the beach next to Jessie, holding up her phone to take a picture. "It'll be nice and warm when you get in."

Dad sighed. "That's because we'll be so numb with cold we won't be able to feel it! Come on, Anya—let's run." He grabbed Anya's hand and they dashed into the water. It *was* cold. Freezing. But Mom was right. After a couple of minutes, it really didn't feel cold at all.

They had the best morning playing and splashing around with the body-board, Dad swimming along, towing Anya behind him, and jumping in and out of the waves. Then Dad helped Anya build a sand castle that was even bigger than the one she and Rachel and the others had made the day before.

After lunch, Jessie was fussing and a bit cranky, so Mom and Dad took turns playing with her and carrying her up and down the beach, trying to persuade her she wanted a nap. She didn't, though. She kept on crying, and Anya knew there was no use asking Dad if he wanted to go in the sea again. She lay on her front on the sun-warmed pebbles, reading her book.

By about three o'clock, Mom was starting to look really anxious. Even Anya was feeling worried—her little sister looked so miserable. "Mom, should we go back to the cottage?" she suggested, looking at Jessie's scarlet cheeks. "Maybe Jessie just doesn't want to sleep in her stroller. If we went back you could put her down in the crib and she might feel better."

"Would you mind?" Mom asked, looking at Anya gratefully. "I don't want to spoil your beach day, Anya. We've only got a week here. Maybe Dad could stay with you and I'll take Jessie back."

"I'd rather come with you," Anya said, with one quick, wistful glance at the sea. "I've got that bead-jewelry kit Nana bought me for the vacation; I'd like to do some of that. And anyway, I think it's going to rain." She didn't, really—there was only one tiny cloud in the sky—but she wanted to make Mom feel better.

They started to pack up, folding the blanket and gathering all their bits and pieces together. As they were walking along the promenade to the cliff path, Anya stopped for a last look at the sea. *It'll still be there tomorrow*, she told herself. *And I bet Jessie will feel better by then. Maybe Mom will go in the sea with me. Rachel might be back on the beach, too.* She was just about to turn around and run after her mom and dad, when she saw a dog—a little golden, curly-haired dog—trotting along the promenade a short way behind her.

"That looks just like Molly," Anya muttered to herself. She squinted thoughtfully at the little dog. "But it can't be. I haven't seen Rachel and the others. And I did look all the way down the beach when we arrived."

"Anya! Come on!" Dad called, waving to her.

Anya turned to wave back. "Coming!" she answered. But then she looked at the dog again. She was almost certain it was Molly—the dark eyes were just the same, and the messy curls around her muzzle and ears. "It *is* her! Molly, what are you doing here on your own?" Even if she *had* just missed Rachel's family and they were here after all, Molly was too far away from them now. Had she run off?

"They should keep you on a leash," Anya murmured worriedly. She glanced over at Dad, who was starting to look a bit upset. She'd have to go and explain. Anya dashed along the promenade to where he was waiting at the bottom of the path. Mom had already set off with the stroller.

"Come on, sweetheart. We really need to get home. Mom wants to give Jessie some teething gel—she thinks she's got a tooth coming through."

"Dad, can we stop? I just saw Molly— you know, Rachel's dog? She's back there and Rachel's not here. I think Molly's lost."

Dad glanced worriedly up the path. "Are you sure, Anya? This isn't a good time to stop…"

"I know! But I'm really worried. What if something happens to her? If she goes up the path she could end up on the road."

Dad sighed. "All right. You go and see if you can get her to come to you. I'll text your mom and tell her what's happening."

Anya dropped her bag of swimming things and raced back through the people wandering along the promenade.

"Molly! Molly!" she cried, looking around for the golden puppy. "She was just here," she murmured, looking at a blue-and-white-painted beach hut. "I'm sure she was just going past this one."

But there was no little dog to be seen, and Molly didn't come when Anya called.

"Did you find her?" Dad asked, catching up with Anya.

"No!" she said. "And I'm sure it was Molly, Dad, I really am. What will I say to Rachel, Zach, and Lily? I should have gone after her at once."

"They're probably farther down the beach somewhere and she's gone back to them," Dad said soothingly. "Don't panic, Anya."

"But they're *not* here," said Anya, trying not to let her voice wobble. "I've looked. And their mom said they were probably going to an adventure park today. They must have left Molly behind at their cottage and she slipped out somehow. I don't know what to do!"

"Well, at the moment, there isn't anything we can do. Besides, you might just have mistaken another dog for Molly. There are a lot of dogs on the beach—it's one of the nice things about Saltmere. I mean, look. That little spaniel over there seems quite like the dog you were playing with yesterday."

Anya looked over eagerly to where Dad was pointing, hoping that he'd spotted Molly. But it wasn't—the spaniel was cute and curly eared, but it had much darker fur than the golden-haired puppy, and it wasn't all frizzy and curly.

"She's just disappeared," Anya said sadly. "Oh, Molly, where are you?"

Chapter Four

Molly pattered along the seafront, sniffing for food. A little boy had given her half a sandwich at lunchtime, but then his mom had told him off and shooed her away. Half a sandwich was not enough to fill her up, and now she felt empty and miserable.

There was a delicious smell coming from somewhere up ahead—so good that Molly couldn't stop her tail wagging in delight. She hurried along, sniffing hopefully and trying to figure out where the food was.

A family was sitting outside one of the beach huts, eating their fish and chips out of a basket. It smelled so good that Molly felt her mouth water a little. She crept up closer, her tail trembling from side to side in a shy wag. She sat down next to a girl who was sitting in a canvas chair and looked up at her. She glanced between the girl and the fish and chips, her dark brown eyes pleading. *Please can I have some?*

The girl giggled, peeked over at her mom and dad to check that they weren't looking, and sneaked Molly a chip.

"You're so cute," she whispered. "I

bet you're not allowed those, though. Where's your owner gone? Did you slip your leash?" she added, giving Molly another chip.

"Is that a dog, Ella?" her mom called over.

"Yes, look, isn't she lovely?"

"I hope you're not feeding her!"

"Oh, no, 'course I'm not." Ella grinned down at Molly. "Our little secret," she whispered. "But they'll see if I give you any more—sorry."

Suddenly, there was a wild flurry of barking and a big golden Labrador surged out from under one of the chairs, almost overturning the man who was sitting in it. He yelled loudly, and Molly backed away in horror, turning tail and running as the huge Labrador raced after her. He was much bigger than she was, and his legs were a lot longer, too. Even though he'd gotten caught up in all the chairs, he was soon right on her tail, barking and growling furiously. She had been bothering his people.

Molly raced along the promenade as fast as she could, but she didn't have very much energy—not like the Labrador, who was fit and well fed. He caught her, knocking her down with one of his massive paws and rolling her on the concrete. He stood over her, growling and showing his massive teeth, and Molly whimpered with fear, her paws in the air, trying to show that she wouldn't fight. She was sorry—he was in charge.

"George! Get off!" The man who'd nearly been tipped over and the nice girl came racing up.

"Get off that poor little dog!" the girl shrieked.

"Bad dog, George!" The man grabbed George's collar and dragged him away from Molly.

"Awww, she's so scared, poor little thing," the girl said, crouching down by Molly. "Where's your owner? We'd better go and take you back and say sorry that George chased you."

"I'm not sure she's got an owner," the man said, still trying to hold George back. The big dog was growling and trying to lunge at Molly. "George, stop it! No!" he said firmly, and George edged away, with muttery growls. "I think I saw her the other day by the ice-cream kiosk. Maybe she's a stray? But she's such a nice little dog. I'd be surprised if people weren't looking for her."

Molly peered sideways at the big Labrador and realized that he wasn't about to chase her again. She sprang up, trembling, and backed away, step by step.

"Oh, no, come back!" the girl cried. "We need to find out who you belong to!"

But Molly was already gone. As soon as she'd gotten far enough from George, she whipped around and ran away down the promenade, darting behind beach huts so that she was hidden. She could hear the girl calling behind her, but that big dog was there. She couldn't go back.

Anya sat at the kitchen table with her bead kit, listening to Jessie fussing upstairs and still worrying about the puppy.

"Oh, no," she muttered, looking at the bracelet she was threading. She had done it wrong again— for about the third time. She just couldn't concentrate. Anya was sure it had been Molly she'd seen on the beach. She kept wondering if the little dog had gotten home yet. Maybe Rachel and her family were out looking for her—if only she could go and tell them where she'd last seen Molly, it might help. But she didn't even know where Rachel's vacation cottage was.

Anya stood up and went over to the window. At least it was still light. The only time that she remembered being lost herself was a few years before, when she had been Christmas shopping with Mom. She had stopped to look at a beautiful window display, with a toy Santa Claus that waved. She had been transfixed—and then she had turned around to point Santa Claus out and her mom had gone.

It had been late afternoon and getting dark—just the right time to see all the sparkling Christmas lights, but the darkness had made Anya feel even more scared.

Mom had found her, of course. She had only gone on a few steps up the street before she realized that Anya wasn't right beside her anymore. She'd come dashing back and scooped Anya up and hugged her. But Anya still remembered that panicked moment in the dark when she thought that she was lost forever. Now she wondered if Molly was feeling the same way. She turned around from the window and marched determinedly up the stairs. Mom and Dad were trying to give Jessie some teething gel, but she kept spitting it out.

"Oh, hello, love." Mom looked up at her worriedly. "Are you all right, Anya? Do you want to grab an apple or some cheese and crackers or something? I'm really sorry—we haven't even started making dinner yet. It's going to be a while."

"It's OK, Mom, I'm not hungry. I was just wondering if I could walk down to the beach and look at the sea. I won't be long—it's turned this beautiful blue color and I want to see it closer."

Their cottage went straight out onto the path along the top of the cliff, so there were no roads to cross. Anya crossed her fingers hopefully behind her back. She hated lying to Mom and Dad, but she wasn't really lying, she told herself. The sea *was* that lovely color and she would look at it—it was just that she would be looking for a little curly-haired dog *more*. If she'd said that she was going out to search for Molly, she was pretty sure Dad would say no—

he hadn't been that pleased when she'd made him spend ages looking for her earlier on.

"I'll be back by the time you've gotten dinner ready—or I could come back and help make it. Do you want me to turn the oven on or anything?" Anya suggested.

Dad sighed. "At this rate we'll be heading out to the fish-and-chip shop, Anya. Don't worry. Be back soon, all right? And no talking to strangers."

"I promise." Anya ran into her room to grab a cardigan and raced back downstairs and out the door before they could change their minds.

Chapter Five

"Molly! Molly!"

Molly was curled up under the beach huts, where she'd run after the huge Labrador had chased her. She had been so frightened that she felt shaky, and for ages she couldn't stop panting. Her tail was still tucked tightly between her legs, and she had curled herself into the smallest ball she could, right at the back of the beach hut where it stood against the cliff wall. Exhausted, she'd fallen into an uneasy sleep, twitching as the big dog ran after her in her dreams.

She woke up with a start, feeling puzzled. Was someone calling her? She was almost sure she'd heard her name. Her ears pricked up—as much as her frizzy, curly ears ever did—and she listened intently. But there was no one there. Molly sighed and turned around a few times on the dusty, sandy concrete, trying to go back to sleep. She would wait a while longer before she trotted down to her comfy hollow in the grass. She wanted to make sure that the Labrador really was gone.

Molly laid her nose down on her paws and tried to ignore how hungry she felt—a few chips didn't go far. She was just starting to snooze when she heard the voice again. She was sure this time. Someone *was* calling her name!

Molly wriggled forward under the beach hut, until she could see out from behind the little steps at the front.

Standing on the promenade was a girl—the girl she had played with on the beach, who had given her a biscuit!

"Molly! Molly! Please come out!"

Molly yelped and scrabbled her way

from behind the steps, darting across the promenade to Anya.

"Molly! You're here! Oh, it really is you! I was right." Anya rubbed the excited little dog's ears and laughed as Molly danced around her. "Oh, Molly, you're so messy! Look, you're all covered in sand and dirt. I'm so glad I found you—I thought maybe I'd imagined it and it hadn't been you I saw at all." Then she stopped and frowned. "But it's all very well finding you, Moll. We've still got to get you home, and I don't know where Rachel and the others are staying." Anya sat down on the edge of the promenade with her feet in the sand and her arm around Molly.

Molly licked Anya's face, delighted that she could reach it properly now.

"Ugh, Molly!" Anya rubbed it off and gave the puppy a hug. "All Rachel said was that your cottage was really close to the ice-cream shop—the same one where I got my bodyboard. She said it was great, because they were always going past it, and if they all begged, her mom almost always said yes... So I suppose we'll just have to go and have a look around there. Maybe we'll see Rachel or Lily or Zach looking out of a window or something. She gazed down at Molly doubtfully. "I wish I had a leash for you, sweetheart. I don't really want to take you over the road without holding on to you properly." She shuddered at the thought of Molly dashing out in front of a car. "Mom and Dad make enough fuss about *me* crossing roads, even if they do let me walk most of the way home from school now." She looked around, hoping for a bit of string or something that she could tie through Molly's tattered collar.

"Oh! Your collar! Maybe you've got Rachel's mom's or dad's number on there. Let's hope it's a cell …" She turned the collar around carefully, looking for the tag. Molly's fur was matted underneath it and Anya bit her lip. She really liked Rachel's family, but she didn't think they were great at looking after Molly. The poor little dog needed a really good brush—probably a trim from a proper dog groomer, too. "No tag… It's just got *Molly* woven on as part of the collar. That's no good. Oh, well, maybe the tag with the number came off." Anya sighed. "Back to Plan A, then." She was just looking at a heap of seaweed and wondering if she could twist it together to make a sort of rope, when she rolled her eyes. "I'm so stupid, Molly. My scarf!"

Anya was wearing a pretty flowered bandanna that Mom had bought her to wear over her hair instead of a sunhat. She pulled it off and undid the knot, stretching it out. It wasn't that long, but it would be OK if she bent down a bit.

"Here, Molly. A nice new leash, look." She tied one corner of the bandanna through the strong metal ring on Molly's collar and stood up, keeping a tight hold on the other end. "That'll do... Come on, Molly! Let's go and take you home!"

Molly walked along beside Anya as they headed up the stepped path to the top of the cliff. She sniffed happily at the clumps of wild plants that were growing out over the concrete steps, and Anya smiled down at her proudly. She was so lovely, even if she was a bit scruffy. As they walked along the seafront path, Anya couldn't help pretending to herself that Molly was her own dog. She could imagine it for five minutes, couldn't she?

But the walk to the ice-cream shop was far too short. Soon Anya was standing outside and staring at the closed shutters. If it had still been open, she could have run in to ask if they happened to know where Rachel's family was staying, seeing as Rachel reckoned they were the shop's best customers.

"There're a lot of houses along here, Molly," Anya murmured, looking quickly around at the town square, surrounded by cottages. "I suppose I'm just going to have to ring the doorbells and ask." But she stood on the grassy patch for a little while, hoping she'd suddenly spot Rachel. She hated the thought of having to ask at all those houses. She'd told Mom and Dad she wouldn't talk to strangers, for a start. And what if Rachel's family wasn't even staying in one of them? Maybe they were in one of the streets close to the town square?

Anya sighed. She was just going to have to be brave. She marched over to the nearest house and rang the bell. There were buckets and spades in the little doorway, so at least there were children there.

The door opened and Anya found herself staring at a boy a bit older than her—but it definitely wasn't Zach. And there was a littler boy peering around him, too.

"Oh! Sorry! Wrong house," Anya stammered. "Um, I don't suppose you know where Zach and Rachel are staying, do you?"

"No," the boy said, staring at her as though she was mad.

"Sorry…" Anya backed away and gently tugged Molly after her.

"I should have explained why I was asking," Anya muttered to Molly as they went on to the next house. "Oh, that was so embarrassing."

No one answered at the following two houses—which Anya was secretly relieved about. The next door was opened by a friendly looking lady, who smiled at Molly and said, "Oh, what a sweet dog."

"She isn't mine," Anya said, grateful that the lady had made it easy for her to explain. "I found her on the beach, but I know who she belongs to and I'm pretty sure they're staying around here. They told me they were in a cottage by the ice-cream shop. No one's asked about a dog, have they? There are three children—a boy and two girls."

The lady looked at the houses around the town square thoughtfully. "It's very nice of you to try to bring her home. I wonder if it's Mrs. Merritt's family.

I know they were staying with her, and she does have three grandchildren. She told me she was going to have trouble squashing them and their dog all in, especially now that her grandson's so tall."

"Oh!" Anya said delightedly. "That sounds right! Zach is really tall. Where does she live, please?"

"That white house over there on the corner. Good luck! If you don't find her owners, do you know where the vet's office is? I'm sure they'd help you out—it's on the main street."

"Thanks!" Anya beamed at her. "Come on, Molly." She patted her leg, and Molly scampered after her across the town square to the white house. Anya hurried up the little path between the bright flower beds and rang the doorbell firmly, not feeling as nervous as she had before. She was sure this had to be the right place, even though Rachel hadn't mentioned that they were staying with their grandma.

The door took a long time to be answered, though. Wasn't that a bit odd? Wouldn't Rachel or Zach or Lily have run to get it? Perhaps they were out? In fact, they were probably out looking for Molly. Anya sighed and pressed the bell one last time, just in case.

The door swung open sharply and a very angry-looking elderly lady stared out at Anya.

"What is it? Couldn't you tell that I was coming? I was asleep—so rude!"

"Oh … Oh, I'm really sorry." Anya backed away and so did Molly, with a little whimper. "The lady across the road thought this might be your grandchildren's dog—she said they were staying with you."

"Of course it isn't. They have a Jack Russell. And they went home yesterday. Silly woman."

"I'm really sorry—I didn't mean to wake you up. I was just trying to find the dog's owners, that's all." Anya swallowed, trying not to cry. The old lady seemed so grumpy.

"Hmm. Well, I hope you find them." The old lady looked slightly less annoyed. "There are children in the house two doors down, that way—why don't you try there?"

Anya nodded. "Thank you," she said, hurrying off as fast as she could and ringing the bell at the house the old lady had pointed to.

She had to stand on the step for a few moments, but when the door opened, it was worth the wait. "Thank goodness it's you!" she gasped, as Rachel peered around the door in front of her.

Chapter Six

"Have you come to see us? It's Anya," Rachel called back into the house. "My friend from the beach, Mom." Rachel smiled at Anya and then looked down at Molly. "Oh! You've brought Molly, too."

She looked a little bit puzzled, Anya thought. "Hadn't you noticed that she was gone?" she asked Rachel. Molly had been out since the middle of the afternoon! It did seem strange that they hadn't noticed.

Rachel frowned. "Gone where?"

"She was running along the beach this afternoon, but I couldn't catch her," Anya explained. "I told Mom and Dad I was going down to the sea so I could have another look for her. She must have slipped out earlier on—or maybe you left her on the beach," she added doubtfully. She couldn't imagine being that careless, but Rachel didn't seem to have a clue where her dog was …

"We haven't been to the beach," Rachel said slowly. "We went to an adventure park. We've only just gotten back."

Anya nodded. "She slipped out, then."

She crouched down and rubbed Molly's poor scruffy ears that needed brushing so badly. She was almost tempted not to give Molly back …

Rachel crouched down, too, and Molly sniffed her fingers in a friendly sort of way. Anya watched, frowning a little. Molly didn't seem that excited to see her owner.

"Anya, I don't understand." Rachel looked at her over Molly's head. "Why would we notice Molly had gone? And gone *where*?"

"Don't you care about her at all?" Anya felt her eyes filling with tears. How could Rachel not even be worried that Molly had been out on her own all day? She could have been run over! "She's your dog! You're supposed to look after her!"

Rachel simply stared at her for a moment. Then she shook her head. "No, she isn't," she said slowly.

"What?"

"She's not our dog, Anya." Rachel frowned. "She doesn't belong to us. We don't even *have* a dog."

"But she was with you on the beach!"

Anya looked down at Molly, who was watching them anxiously.

The little dog wagged her tail, very faintly. She could tell they were getting upset with each other, Anya realized, and she patted Molly's ears gently. "It's OK," she murmured. Then she looked up at Rachel. "She's really not yours? I was so sure… She was with us all of that afternoon. And you knew her name— you told me she was called Molly!"

"Yes, because it's on her collar." Rachel pointed to the name, woven into the fabric. "She was watching us playing in the sea and then she just tagged along. She was so gorgeous—but I thought she belonged to those teenage boys who were sitting farther up the beach. I was sure she did." Rachel frowned. "I thought they were mean, not playing with her... And they didn't seem to mind her being with us, so I just kept fussing over her."

"Oh, wow," Anya muttered. "I suppose I just thought she was yours because of the way you apologized about her knocking over my tower. Sorry," she added. "I was really telling you off just now. You must have thought I was mad!"

"That's all right," said Rachel. "I would have done the same if I thought you weren't looking after your dog. But how did you find us? I never told you the address of the cottage, did I? I wished I'd thought of giving you Mom's cell number, so we could meet up on the beach again. I was so angry with myself last night when I realized I couldn't even call you!"

Anya sighed. "You told me you were staying near the ice-cream shop, so I knocked on doors. It was embarrassing. And the old lady two doors down was really angry with me!"

"Ooooh, she exploded at Lily the other day because she spilled sand out of her bucket onto the pavement. I think she's just a bit grumpy. It's not your fault." Rachel put her arm around Anya's shoulders and gave her a hug. "I'm sorry you got into trouble."

Anya smiled at her, but then her smile faded. "It doesn't matter—but, Rachel, if Molly doesn't belong to you, then whose dog *is* she?"

"I don't know." Rachel looked worriedly at Molly. "I suppose I just thought she belonged to those boys, the same way you thought she was ours. I never actually saw them call her or anything ..."

"Do you think she could be a stray and that maybe she doesn't belong to anyone? She's ever so scruffy. Sorry, Molly, you're beautiful, but you *are* scruffy," Anya told her. "I mean, she needs grooming really badly, and she's covered in sand."

"She's too thin, as well," Rachel pointed out.

Anya ran her hand over Molly's domed head, and Molly panted at her happily. "So—do you think she's a stray?"

"Maybe …" Rachel nodded. "It seems that way, doesn't it?"

"Poor Molly," Anya whispered. "I wonder what happened—she's so lovely and she's still only a puppy."

"Perhaps she got lost when her owners were here on vacation," Rachel suggested sadly. "And they went home without her."

"That's awful …" Anya swallowed. "What am I going to do? I thought I was bringing her home and now it seems she doesn't have a home at all."

"Rachel, are you two all right out there?" Rachel's mom came out of the kitchen. "Hello, Anya. That's a sweet little dog. You had her with you on the beach, didn't you?"

Rachel and Anya looked at each other and started to laugh. "Mom, Anya thought Molly was ours. She brought her back! And now we don't know who she belongs to."

"Oh!" Anya looked down at her watch. "I have to get back. I told Mom and Dad I'd only be a few minutes. I was just supposed to be going to look at the sea."

"They'll be terribly worried about you," Rachel's mom said in a horrified sort of voice that made Anya feel much worse. "We'd better take you home at once." She called out that she'd be back soon and closed the front door behind her. Then she hurried the girls and Molly down the street.

"Where are you staying, Anya?" she asked. "Can you remember the way?"

"Oh, yes. It's one of the cottages on the front, by the sea. I can go back by myself, honestly."

But Rachel's mom shook her head. "No, it's all right, I'm sure you could, but I want to make certain that you get home safely."

"Mom," Rachel put in suddenly. "If Molly's a stray, and we think she must be, can we keep her?"

Anya gasped—it was exactly what she had been thinking. If only she had said something first!

But Rachel's mom shook her head firmly. "No, of course not. For a start, the cottage has a no-pets rule. And what would Alfie think if we came home and got him out of the cat kennel and there was a dog in his house? He'd probably walk out!"

Rachel sighed. "I suppose so."

Anya took a deep, shaky breath and wrapped her hand more tightly around Molly's makeshift leash. Until Rachel had spoken, she'd only had the idea in the back of her mind, but how amazing would it be if Molly could be hers? After all, no one else seemed to want her … Why shouldn't they keep her?

"Would you like to stay with me?" she whispered to Molly as she saw their cottage and hurried ahead. "Would you like to be my dog?" She knocked lightly on the front door of the cottage—the last thing she wanted to do was wake up Jessie. She needed Mom and Dad in the best mood possible.

The door swung open at once, and Mom grabbed her into a hug. "Anya, where have you been? You said you'd only be a few minutes. I was about to go out looking for you!"

"Sorry, Mom …"

"Anya's actually been extremely resourceful," Rachel's mom put in. "She found this dog *and* she figured out where we'd been staying, so she could bring the poor little thing back to us. Only the dog isn't actually ours."

"Is that the dog you were looking for earlier, Anya?" Dad asked, peering over Mom's shoulder.

"Yes, but she doesn't belong to the other family. We don't know who she belongs to at all." Anya crouched down and picked Molly up, showing her to Mom and Dad. "She's so lovely I can't see how anybody would abandon her."

"I'm sorry we can't look after her ourselves until her owner is found," Rachel's mom explained. "But we had to sign a no-pets agreement for our cottage."

"I think pets are allowed in this one," Dad said slowly. "But we can't have a dog here—what about Jessie?"

"Molly's really friendly, Dad," Anya explained. "She wouldn't snap at Jessie."

"She was very patient with the children on the beach the other day," Rachel's mom agreed.

"Couldn't we just look after her for a couple of days, Dad?" Anya suggested hopefully. "I could take her to the vet's to see if anyone's reported her lost. And put posters up about her."

She didn't say what she was really thinking, which was, *And then if no one knows about her, maybe we can just take her home with us …*

Chapter Seven

Molly was lying on an old picnic blanket that Anya had found in one of the cupboards in the living room. She was very sleepy, mostly because she was full. It was the strangest feeling, not to be hungry. She couldn't remember the last time she hadn't been desperate for food.

Anya and her dad had gone to the

supermarket to get some dog food on their way to the fish-and-chip shop. Jessie had fallen asleep at last, but her tooth was still making her really miserable. Anya had begged Dad to let her buy a comb as well. She wanted to try to get rid of the worst of the tangles from Molly's coat.

So now Molly was well fed and a bit less sandy and scruffy. There were still a lot of knots in her fur, though, because the comb hadn't been up to it and several of its teeth had snapped off.

"I'll buy you a proper dog-grooming brush when I go to the vet tomorrow," Anya had told Molly as she'd hugged her good-night. Then she gave a tiny sigh. "I know I ought to hope that the vet knows who you belong to, but I really don't. I want you to belong to me." She gave Molly one last pat and went off upstairs.

Molly stared after her, wondering where Anya was going. She stayed on her blanket, but she kept her eyes on the stairs, watching until she fell asleep. She woke again a couple of hours later to find the house dark and quiet. She was all alone downstairs.

Molly lay on the blanket for a long while, with her head on her front paws. She was still very sleepy, but she wanted to know where everyone was. Molly had lived without an owner for months now, and it had felt so good to have Anya fussing over her. She had enjoyed having her fur combed, too, even when the comb caught in all the tangles and pulled. Somebody wanted her. Somebody cared enough about her to tidy her up and make her a comfy bed.

Molly got up and went to sniff at the bottom of the stairs. They were all up there, she thought. All of a sudden, Molly was desperate to see that Anya hadn't disappeared. It had happened before, after all ... People had gone away and left her. Quickly, she padded up the stairs, sniffing for Anya's room. She found it almost at once, poking her nose around the door.

Anya turned over as her bedroom

door creaked open and peered sleepily at the puppy. "Hello, Molly!" she whispered. "Did you come to find me? Aren't you clever? Oh, you're such a good dog."

Molly scurried over to the bed. Anya leaned down to pat her and make a fuss. "Molly, come on," she murmured. "Come on up here, good dog ... That's it!" She giggled delightedly as Molly scrambled up onto the end of the bed and curled up blissfully by her feet. It was just the way she'd dreamed having a dog would be.

"So, they didn't leave a number?" Anya asked the vet's receptionist. She hated it that Molly's owners didn't seem to have looked after her properly. Even though the receptionist was almost sure that the people she remembered coming in to ask about their lost dog had been talking about Molly, she said they were in a rush and hadn't left her their phone number. Molly wasn't microchipped, either.

Secretly, though, Anya couldn't help feeling relieved. If the vet did have a way to contact Molly's real owners, Anya would have to give her back. And that was getting harder and harder to imagine.

"There's an animal shelter in Westerby," the receptionist went on, handing Anya a leaflet. "I'm afraid we can't take stray dogs here, although I'd love to. She looks like a little treasure."

"She is sweet," Anya's dad agreed. "I wouldn't mind keeping her, but we've got a small baby, so I just don't think it's a good idea." He looked over Anya's shoulder at the leaflet. "Mmm. I suppose we'll have to take her there, then. I'd better call your mom."

"Can't we wait a bit?" Anya asked, crossing her fingers in the folds of her skirt and giving her best pleading-eyes look to Dad. "We still don't know for certain that Molly belonged to those people. It could have been another dog. Me and Rachel are going to make notices to put up, to tell everybody that we've found her."

Dad nodded thoughtfully. "Well, I suppose a day or two wouldn't hurt, just so long as your mom agrees," he said. "But after that she'll have to go to the shelter."

Rachel had brought a sketchpad on vacation with her and lots of felt pens, so she and Anya drew posters that afternoon at Anya's cottage. It was a grayish sort of day, not really the best day for playing out on the beach anyway. Then they borrowed Anya's mom's cell, just in case of an emergency, and went out to stick up the signs on lampposts and on the railings along the seafront. "After all, she was on the beach," Rachel pointed out. "So it makes sense that her owners might have lost her there. If they're still looking for her, this is a good place to put a sign."

Too good, Anya thought to herself. She almost felt like tearing the posters down again.

"We've got to get back," Rachel said as they finished putting up the last one. "Mom said she'd come and pick me up from yours at three and it's five to. Oh, do you want to come on a picnic with us tomorrow afternoon? She said it was OK to ask you and your mom and dad, and Jessie and Molly, too."

"Yes, please!" Anya nodded eagerly. "But if we're going on a picnic, then we can't take Molly to the shelter. Dad did say we could keep her for a day or two, though ..."

Rachel sighed. "It's not fair—I wish you could keep her. She loves you!"

Anya giggled. "Only because I feed her loads and she's so hungry. I think she looks fatter already, and we've only had her a day."

"It isn't just that. She looks so happy. And gorgeous, now that you've brushed her and she's got a new collar and leash."

Anya had spent most of her vacation money at the vet's, buying things for Molly. But she didn't mind. Even if Molly did go to the shelter, she was much more likely to be adopted if she was well groomed and had a nice collar on, wasn't she? Anya hated the thought of Molly being stuck at the shelter for ages, with nobody to stroke her and fuss over her and love her properly. *Like I would*, she added silently to herself.

Rachel's mom was just coming along the seafront path as they got to Anya's cottage. They waved to her.

"Thanks for inviting us on the

picnic," Anya said. "I'll just run in and ask Mom and Dad, shall I? Oh, dear…" She made a face. "I can hear Jessie crying—she's teething."

Dad came to let her in. "Sorry about the noise," he said to Rachel's mom, with a frazzled sort of smile. "Poor Jess. She's really miserable. Anya's mom is upstairs catching up on a bit of sleep."

Rachel's mom started to explain about the picnic, and Anya and Rachel went over to see Jessie. She was in her car seat—it looked like Dad had been rocking her. Her cheeks were red, and she was making sad little hiccupping noises.

"Hello, Jessie," Anya crooned. "Are your teeth still hurting? Poor baby …" And she rocked the car seat gently.

Rachel and Molly watched, but the rocking didn't seem to help—Jessie's crying only got louder.

"It's OK, Molly," Rachel whispered, seeing the dog's ears twitching worriedly. "I don't think Molly likes the noise."

Anya looked around, wondering if she should move Molly away from Jessie, but the little dog crept forward and laid her nose very gently on the car seat. She gave a quiet whine and stared at Jessie.

Jessie stared back, looking surprised—at least, Anya thought she did. It was hard to tell with babies sometimes. But she definitely stopped crying. She gazed into Molly's dark eyes and made a sort of cooing sound.

Dad looked down at Jessie and smiled. "That's the first time she's stopped fussing all afternoon!" he murmured. "Good girl, Molly. She's been very good around Jessie, actually," he explained to Rachel's mom. "I was worried about having a dog with a baby, but maybe if we were very careful …"

Anya and Rachel exchanged a delighted look. Molly was definitely winning Dad over!

"Mom and Dad are still making sandwiches, so they sent us to get you," Zach explained.

"OK, I'll go and tell Mom and Dad you're here. I don't think they're quite ready. Can you put Molly's leash on, Rachel?" Anya handed Rachel the leash, and Molly wriggled and yapped, trying to catch it in her teeth. She loved walks.

Dad came down the stairs and laughed at Molly jumping around. "Poor Moll, you can't make her wait now, Anya—she might keel over from the excitement. Why don't the two of you walk over with Zach and Rachel, and we'll catch up with you in a minute?"

Rachel went to hand the leash back to Anya when they got out of the front door, but Anya shook her head. "You can hold her if you want to," she told Rachel. She knew how much Rachel would love a dog, even though she adored Alfie, their little ginger cat. She'd shown Anya pictures of him. He had the brightest pink nose Anya had ever seen on a cat.

They walked to Rachel and Zach's house along the seafront path, past lots of other people with dogs and children who stopped to stroke her. Anya watched Molly proudly—she looked so lovely, and she was walking nicely for Rachel, too.

Molly trotted along, sniffing happily at all the good smells along the bottom of the railings and enjoying the fuss that the children were making of her. It was so nice to be patted and told she was a good dog.

She glanced up at Anya to check that she was still there and hadn't disappeared, and then looked ahead to see where they were going. She stopped short with a frightened whimper. She knew that dog. That big, fierce golden dog who was coming toward them.

He'd spotted her, too, and he growled loudly, pulling hard on his leash. The dog was going to chase her again!

Molly whimpered loudly and darted backward, nearly tripping Rachel. Zach and Anya both made a grab for her leash to help, but Molly yanked it out of Rachel's hand and shot across the road, desperate to get away from the big Labrador.

A car stopped suddenly and the driver started to yell at the three children, but they were already darting across the road behind him, racing after Molly.

Chapter Eight

"I'm really sorry!" Rachel gasped. "I didn't mean to let go—she pulled so hard!"

"It wasn't your fault," Anya panted back. "She was really scared of that Labrador. I don't know why. She didn't mind any of the other dogs."

"We're really close to our house," Zach said. "She did go down here, didn't she? I reckon she's got to be on the town square somewhere."

Anya nodded. There was a cold feeling in her stomach, and she was trying hard not to cry. Just when Dad had started to think about keeping Molly! She'd heard him talking to Mom about it the night before—about how good Molly was and how responsible Anya was being, trying to look after the puppy and find her owners. They wouldn't think Anya was responsible now that Molly had gotten lost again!

"We'll find her," Zach said. "Don't worry. Come on."

They raced across the little town square, looking around and calling.

"At least she's got her leash on," Anya

said, her voice wobbling. "If anyone spots her, they'll know she's slipped away. They might even be able to grab the leash."

"Shall I get Mom and Dad and Lily to come and look, too?" Zach suggested.

"No, I'm sure she went running over the town square," Rachel said. "If we stop and get Mom and Dad she might go somewhere else. We need to find her now!"

Anya nodded. Rachel was right. "Molly!" she called, her voice squeaky with fright. "Molly, come on! Come on, sweetheart!" Then she gave a little gasp. "Oh! The dog treats—I brought a packet with me, to be her part of the picnic. I got them at the vet's for her." She rummaged in her pocket and pulled out the foil packet. Then she shook it gently, so that the treats rattled around inside. "Here, Molly! Yummy treats, come on!"

She shook them again, but Molly didn't come. "I was sure she'd want them…" Anya whispered. "I don't think she's here. She must have run down to the next road."

"No! Look, I can see her!" Rachel grabbed Anya's arm. "Isn't that her, over in that garden? I'm sure I saw something move just then when you shook the treats."

Anya looked over and saw a pale shape curled up under a fuschia bush. "It is her!" she whispered. "Oh, you star, Rachel. Don't run!" she added to Zach, who looked as though he was about to dash into the garden. "She's really scared. She might race off again."

"OK." Zach nodded. "You creep up and call her."

"Molly …" Anya called gently. "Molly, come here, sweetheart." She gave the bag of treats another shake.

Molly looked up, a little golden face surrounded by the pink and purple flowers. She looked gorgeous—except that she was trembling.

"It's all right," Anya called, standing by the wall. "Come on." She patted her knees gently and Molly crept a touch closer. But she didn't get up and run to Anya.

Anya glanced at the house and hoped the owners wouldn't mind if she went into their garden. She walked onto the path and bent down. "Come on, Moll ..."

This time, Molly wriggled out from under the bush. She crept over to Anya, her head down, still shaking.

"Poor Molly," Anya murmured as she gripped the leash tightly and rubbed Molly's trembling ears. "That big dog really scared you, didn't he?"

Suddenly, Molly jerked on her leash again and Anya glanced around. The front door was opening—and a familiar-looking elderly lady glared out at her.

"Oh, no." Anya breathed. It was the same lady she'd woken up a couple of days before. "I'm sorry," she said out loud. "I didn't mean to disturb you. Molly got scared by another dog and ran away and then she hid under your flowers. We're just going." She could see Mom and Dad coming up the road now, with Jessie in her stroller. She really hoped they weren't going to be mad.

The old lady frowned. "But wasn't it you who came to the door a couple of days ago?"

"Yes," Anya admitted, feeling glad that Rachel and Zach had come over to stand by the wall now.

"Anya thought Molly was ours," Rachel explained. "But she isn't. No one knows who she belongs to, but Anya's looking after her. It was my fault she's in your garden. I let go of her leash." She looked over apologetically at Anya's mom and dad, who had arrived at the house. "I'm sorry, I should have held her tighter."

"But you're all OK?" Anya's dad asked worriedly. "We only saw that you were trying to call Molly out of the garden."

"We're fine," Anya said. "Molly got scared by a big dog. I think she might have met him before—it was like she knew him and he really frightened her."

"I saw your posters," the old lady broke in suddenly. "I didn't realize it was the same dog. I have seen her before, you know, now that I look at her properly."

"Have you?" Anya gulped, wondering if the old lady knew who Molly's owners were. She crouched down and put her arms round the little dog. What if she was about to lose Molly again?

"On the beach. Yes, I'm sure it was her. Two or three times over the summer and never with the same people."

"So she's definitely a stray?" Anya's mom said slowly, looking over at her dad.

The old lady nodded. "Poor little thing—I don't think she belongs to anyone."

Mom smiled at Anya. "I don't think that's true, Anya, do you?"

Anya took a deep breath of relief and smiled shakily back at her mom. Then she buried her nose in Molly's frizzy ears. Molly nuzzled her damp nose against Anya's cheek.

Then she looked up at the old lady and shook her head. "She does," she explained. "Now she belongs to me."

Anya curled up on the chair in front of Mom's computer and carefully typed in Rachel's email address. Mom had written it down in her diary, so she couldn't possibly lose it.

To: Rachel
From: Anya
Subject: Molly!

Hi, Rachel!

I can't believe the summer vacation is nearly over! Do you go back to school next week, like we do?

Me and Mom took Molly to the vet yesterday and the vet said she was gorgeous. He said Molly was probably a mixture of a poodle and something else, that's why she's so curly!

The vet said we have to be very careful with Molly's thick fur—we're going to have to take her to get clipped at a special dog hair salon! She's got a microchip now, so even if she gets lost again, we'll get her back. And we went to get a tag for her collar with Mom's and Dad's numbers on, too! This is a photo of Molly with her tag on. I feel like she's really ours now!

Lots of love from me and Molly—and Molly says hi to Alfie.

Anya

Anya pressed SEND and looked down at Molly, who was curled up under the desk, waiting for her to finish. Molly looked so beautiful now, with her coat clean and brushed. She was definitely less skinny, too.

Molly jumped up, putting her front paws on Anya's knees, her fluffy golden tail wagging. She then rested her chin on Anya's lap and stared up at her adoringly.

"It was the best vacation ever," Anya whispered down to her, stroking Molly's curly ears. "But it's so nice to be home, isn't it—especially now that it's your home, too."

Read them all!